Xmas. 2002

Casey...
"Talky" Baby Boy, we love you.
G. & G. Gamlen

Little Rabbit and the Sea

Written and Illustrated by Gavin Bishop

North-South Books · New York · London

Little Rabbit had never seen the sea.

But every night he dreamed of being a sailor.

"What is the sea like?" he asked his grandmother. "Wild and quiet," she said. "A bit of both."

He asked his father, "What is the sea *really* like?"
"Blue and wide," he said. "Never ending."

"Is the sea wild and quiet or blue and wide?"
Little Rabbit asked his uncle.
"I'd say it's dark and salty," said his uncle.
"Like cider vinegar."

All day long Little Rabbit thought about the sea.

And every night in his dreams he sailed in his little boat with the wind in his ears.

Then one day Little Rabbit heard a "Squark, squark!" A seagull swooped overhead.

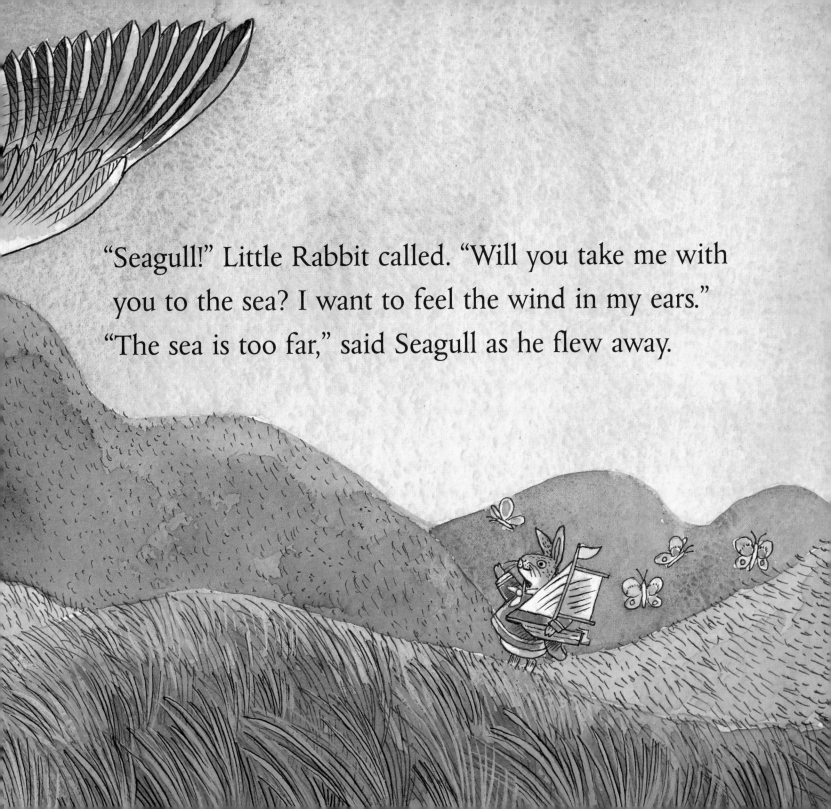

"Seagull!" Little Rabbit called. "Will you take me with you to the sea? I want to feel the wind in my ears." "The sea is too far," said Seagull as he flew away.

Now Little Rabbit longed for the sea even more.

Many weeks later he again heard "Squark, squark!" He looked up and saw Seagull with something in his mouth.

Seagull dropped a big seashell at Little Rabbit's feet.
"Inside this shell is the never-ending sea," he said.

Little Rabbit took the shell.

He raced to the top of the highest hill.

There, with the wind in his ears,
he heard the sea—
and it *was* wild and quiet,

and it *was* blue and wide,

and it *was* dark and salty like cider vinegar.

For Vivien

Published in the United States by North-South Books Inc., New York.

Published simultaneously in Great Britain, Canada, Australia, and
New Zealand in 1997 by North-South Books, an imprint of
Nord-Süd Verlag AG, Gossau Zürich, Switzerland.

Library of Congress Cataloging-in-Publication Data is available.
A CIP catalogue record for this book is available from The British Library.

The artwork consists of pen-and-ink and watercolor
Designed by Marc Cheshire

ISBN 1-55858-809-4 (trade binding)
1 3 5 7 9 TB 10 8 6 4 2
ISBN 1-55858-810-8 (library binding)
1 3 5 7 9 LB 10 8 6 4 2
Printed in Belgium

For more information about our books, and the authors and artists
who create them, visit our website at http://www.northsouth.com